BLOOD
SPORT

BLOOD SPORT

Tash McAdam

orca soundings

ORCA BOOK PUBLISHERS

Library and Archives Canada Cataloguing in Publication

Title: Blood sport / Tash McAdam.
Names: McAdam, Tash, author.
Series: Orca soundings.
Description: Series statement: Orca soundings

Identifiers: Canadiana (print) 20190168773 | Canadiana (ebook) 20190168781 |
ISBN 9781459824362 (softcover) | ISBN 9781459824379 (PDF) |
ISBN 9781459824386 (EPUB)

Classification: LCC PS8626.C33 B56 2020 | DDC jc813/.6—dc23

Library of Congress Control Number: 2019943953
Simultaneously published in Canada and the United States in 2020

Summary: In this high-interest novel for teen readers,
Jason is determined to find out the truth about his sister's death.

*Orca Book Publishers is committed to reducing the consumption
of nonrenewable resources in the making of our books. We make
every effort to use materials that support a sustainable future.*

Orca Book Publishers gratefully acknowledges the support for its
publishing programs provided by the following agencies: the Government of
Canada, the Canada Council for the Arts and the Province of British Columbia
through the BC Arts Council and the Book Publishing Tax Credit.

Edited by Tanya Trafford
Design by Ella Collier
Cover images by gettyimages.ca/CarlaMc (front) and
Shutterstock.com/Krasovski Dmitri (back)

ORCA BOOK PUBLISHERS
orcabook.com

Printed and bound in Canada.

23 22 21 20 • 4 3 2 1

For Alex, my big sister

Chapter One

Jason's hands won't stop shaking. He clenches his fists, his sister's silver ring digging into his palm, but they keep shaking. He bursts into tears the second the door finally closes.

He can hear the footsteps of the police officer walking away. The same one who came six weeks ago to inform him of his sister's death.

Door closed and case closed. In front of Jason, on the sad, small bed in the sad, small room, is everything Becca left behind. Two boxes—a whole life—and Jason's hope for a future. He is about to age out of the foster-care system. In four months, when he turns eighteen, he'll be booted out of the group home. Maybe onto the street. Becca was supposed to be here. Becca was supposed to take care of him. But all that's left of Becca are these two boxes.

It's hard to breathe. His binder must be too tight. His chest feels like it's collapsing. It takes him three tries to get his shirt off. He pulls off the material crushing his breasts down flat and throws it on the old blanket on the bed. He feels better, but barely.

Two years on testosterone, male hormones, has changed Jason. It's made his shoulders wider, his jaw bigger and his body hairier. But without a shirt, it is easy to see what he is. A transgender guy. Someone in danger. The staff at the group home know, of course. They take him to get his shots and see his doctors. But if any of the other kids found out, Jason would be in for a world of hurt.

He stands in the middle of the room, his mind full of pain and fear. He feels like he's dying. He can't breathe at all.

After a while the panic attack fades. As he calms down he realizes he's half-naked. It would be *so* bad if someone walked in right now. Running to the bed, he grabs his binder. The door bangs open before he can put it back on.

Panicking, Jason drops the binder and grabs his shirt. If anyone sees his chest, they'll know what he has been hiding. He pulls the shirt over his head, his back still to the door. He prays for his strong shoulders to help him pass. For whoever it is to see just a boy.

"Yo, Jase, saw the pigs came by again. Did they solve your sister's murder yet?" The thick voice can only belong to Derek. Jason hates Derek. The guy is built like a monster and has a personality to match.

It takes everything Jason has in him to sound normal. "Not yet." Ever since he'd yelled at the care worker that his sister couldn't have overdosed, that she never did drugs, not *ever,* the other teens at the care home like to tease him about it. Especially Derek.

Jason's whole body shivers as he wonders whether Derek wants to fight again. Jason's ribs are still bruised from last time. If he stays facing away, his back is open to possible danger. If he turns around, Derek might see his chest under his shirt.

To his relief, Derek just snorts and bangs back out into the hallway. Jason waits until the door shuts behind him and then rushes to it. He kicks the door stopper tightly into place. It's dangerous. In case there's a fire. He's not supposed to have it. They've taken four off him already, but it's the only way he can breathe in this place.

Safely locked in, Jason walks slowly back to the bed. His whole body feels like it's full of rocks. What is he going to do without Becca? How can this be his life now?

Dropping down on the bed, he knocks one of the boxes over. It tips sideways, spilling its contents onto the blankets.

The copy of Sherlock Holmes that falls out makes him gasp. It was their dad's, the collected stories. When he'd lost his job and started drinking, he'd started selling most of his first editions. But Becca had taken this one. First it had been in her bedroom, on the shelf by her bed. Then, after she moved out, it was on display in her apartment, which Jason was going to move into once he left the group home. Part of their plan.

The book is light brown, with gold leaf on the leather cover and gold-edged pages. Becca has read it so often that the creamy cover is dirty. He reaches out to put the book back in the box. He can't face looking through the pieces of her life. But as he picks up the book he realizes there's something wrong. The page edges aren't shiny like they should be. They are dull and brown, no gold in sight. Curious, he picks up the book. He runs his finger down the spine. The cover feels weird in his hand.

He opens the book. As soon as he does, he can see what's wrong. The pages aren't pages at all. The cover of the book has been stuck onto a box. Sherlock Holmes's adventures aren't anywhere to be seen. There are no pages inside. No stories. Instead there are dozens of newspaper clippings.

Missing girls. Reports of missing girls from the Downtown Eastside. Dating back more than two years. The one with the oldest report has a face he vaguely recognizes. Anna Kerov, one of Becca's friends from work. She was a cocktail server, like Becca. Reported missing in 2017.

Why did his sister have these? Why was she collecting, and hiding, reports of missing girls? Jason's heart is beating too fast. His hands are shaking again. Becca must have been mixed up in something bad. Why else would she have this stuff?

Under the clippings there's something else. A flat white square. Not paper. Thicker. It is wedged into the corners of the box, and it takes a bit of effort to wiggle it free.

It's a Polaroid photo. A shot of a street. Two dark figures standing under a neon sign. Even with two letters blown out, Jason can see that it should say

Ray's Place. A pair of red boxing gloves next to the name look like they probably flashed on and off.

What does this all mean? A photo of a boxing gym, in a box full of newspaper articles about missing girls. And now Becca is dead. Jason is more sure than ever that she didn't overdose.

His hand tightens around the photograph and crushes it into a ball.

Chapter Two

Jason has already missed most of this school term, so taking another day off isn't a big deal. He's failing everything and has been for years. Another phone call won't make a difference. Going to class doesn't hold any appeal at the best of times. Right now is definitely not the best of times.

Walking around the Downtown Eastside in sweats and a hoodie, he finds that everything looks normal. Jason keeps the crumpled Polaroid in his hand, hoping to recognize something. Nothing looks like the gray stone of the building in the picture, but he's only been at it for an hour.

Just as he is about to quit and try to find somewhere cheap to grab lunch, he sees it. A dented old neon sign, flickering from bright red to dull gray. Two boxing gloves and a sign that says *Ray's Place*.

Jason had planned to just look. He'd thought maybe he'd find a fast-food place nearby and watch for a while. But his feet take him straight to the building without his brain's permission.

"Hey, kid. You here for open house?" Someone is talking to him from the alley next to the ratty entrance.

"Uh…sure." While his mouth does the talking, his mind demands to know what the heck he thinks he's doing. *It's just a boxing gym. What's the worst that could happen?* he tells it. *Oh yeah, a boxing gym you found out about by digging through your dead sister's murder box!*

A man comes out of the alley and holds out a fist for a bump. Jason taps it and lifts his chin up in greeting. "You box before?" the guy asks, waving Jason up the stairs. He stubs his cigarette out on the wall and follows him.

"Some," Jason replies, nervous energy bubbling in his stomach. He feels a little sick.

Jason hasn't actually boxed before. But he has been in a ton of fights. Being trans usually means someone wants to smash your face in. Jason learned early on that you have to fight back or it just gets worse and worse. His parents used to yell about it, back before his mom died and his dad lost it. After that no one cared about his black eyes or split lips anymore. No one except Becca.

Up the stairs is a big open space with huge old windows. It looks exactly like one of those old-school sweat-stained places in the action movies. Jason expects a crusty military vet to step out of the dark and smirk.

A raised boxing ring dominates the center of the room. The posts and ropes wobble as two guys go at it. The meaty *thud* of their punches echoes through the large space. Looking around the room, Jason sees mats, weights, benches and the occasional torso dummy or free-standing punching bag.

"Yo, Little Jay, we got another fish." The guy who followed Jason up the stairs slaps him on the shoulder so hard that he staggers slightly. Then the guy just strides off.

"What's up, shorty?" A huge dark-skinned man Jason assumes to be

Little Jay—a classic case of nicknames not fitting—is standing in the doorway of a room Jason hadn't even noticed. It looks like it might be a small office of some sort. "Welcome to Ray's. C'mon in and sign your day-one paperwork. Great timing. We have a class starting in a few minutes."

Jason is right—the room is a tiny office. Messy filing cabinets are spilling documents everywhere. He signs the form that Little Jay hands him without really looking at it. His brain isn't working right. He's drifting along without really feeling or doing anything on purpose.

He writes his name on the line, his chosen name. Not the girl's name that still hasn't been changed in the system. Little Jay doesn't ask for any identification. Just his address, social insurance number and date of birth. He fills it all out and then he signs on the dotted line.

"First session's free. After that it's five bucks a workout." The man grins at him, offers him a fist to bump. Jason taps it, and Little Jay waves him out into the gym again. Jason stuffs his hands into his pockets and glances around. His heart pounds, and he wonders what he's doing here, how he let himself get signed up for a class.

"Yo, newbies, hustle up," Little Jay yells, the volume making everyone wince.

About a dozen teens start lining up around the gym, facing Little Jay.

"First, we skip," Little Jay says, a huge grin on his face. "Preet, grab the ropes."

Jason watches a petite girl with big eyes and a tough-looking chin hand out ropes to the group. She keeps one for herself, scowling at Little Jay when he opens his mouth. Jason guesses he was about to tell her to put it back.

And skip they do. Jason skips so long he thinks his wrists might just break off and send his hands flying through the gym. Little Jay talks while they skip.

Some of the kids are making a complete mess of it and keep smacking each other with the ropes, but Jason is an okay skipper. That means he doesn't have to concentrate as hard as the others and can focus on what Little Jay is saying.

"Boxing is hard," Little Jay tells them. "It's hard, and it's sweaty, and you will ache and bruise and curse my name. But if you stick with me, little dudes, I guarantee you'll become something special. It's the perfect sport. Balance, agility, strength, heart."

The session is not all skipping. There are also sprints and footwork drills. And homework. Little Jay tells them that they should all run every day for at least thirty minutes. Finally, when the hour is nearly done, they head to the punching bags. Little Jay lets them whale on them for a while. He pauses by Jason's bag, then slaps him on the shoulder. What is with all these big men hitting him? He will probably have a bruise forming.

"You should come back," Little Jay says to him. "I can see you've got heart, kid."

Despite the fact that Becca's dead, despite everything else shitty going on right now, Jason wants to come back. He's sweaty and tired and sore. But for the first time in six weeks, he's not screaming inside.

Chapter Three

Jason returns to the gym after skipping school again the next day. For one thing, he'd been so caught up in the class the day before that he hadn't done any investigating. But it is more than that. Maybe it's the comforting feeling of his muscles aching from exercise. Maybe it's the good sleep he had—the first one in weeks.

This time he walks into the gym like he belongs there. He sees some of the kids from the day before. He didn't talk to any of them yesterday, but maybe today he will. He drops his hoodie onto one of the wooden benches lining the wall, leaving him in a tight black T-shirt and knee-length shorts. After watching for a moment, he makes his way over to the group.

"What's up," a tall boy says. He scratches the back of his neck under his head covering. A patka, Jason thinks it's called.

"Hey," Jason replies, offering a fist. The boy leans out to bump it. The group shifts a little, making space for Jason to stand with them in a loose circle.

"I'm Sunny," the boy says. Then he gestures at the girl who had fetched the skipping ropes the day before. "This is my sister, Dilpreet."

"Preet," she corrects him, offering her fist to Jason.

He hesitates for a second because girls don't usually want to bump fists. Annoyed with himself, he taps it. She rewards him with a nod and a grin.

"I'm Lucky," the third kid in the group announces. He's a short guy with the sort of checky face Jason would bet gets him in trouble with his teachers often. He's bouncing on the balls of his feet, like he's moving to music Jason can't hear. "You're new, right? I saw you yesterday. Boxing is awesome. I'm going to be a champ! My granddad was a kung fu master back in China." Lucky puts up his fists, shadowboxing playfully.

Jason can't help but let out a soft laugh, because Lucky is tiny. And he's got his thumbs tucked inside his fists.

"I'm Jason," he says, then jerks his chin at Lucky's fists. "Your thumbs should be on the outside. You'll break them like that."

"Oh, new kid knows what's up." A deep voice right behind him makes Jason jump.

"Hey, X." Sunny shifts back as he greets the man, shoving his hands into his pockets.

"Cupcake, there's files that need sorting in the office." He waves a hand in the direction of the room.

Preet twists her mouth to one side like she's got something to say. Sunny kicks her in the back of the calf, quick enough that Jason almost misses it.

Something's making Jason feel uncomfortable. It might be the guy's body language, the way he physically dominates the space. Or maybe it's as simple as him not using Preet's name. Jason can feel anger rising in his chest again. He's been angry since Becca died, ready to break things. His hands are in fists.

The guy looks him up and down. He raises an eyebrow and then snorts. "Looks like everybody's here now." He motions to another group of kids sitting on the bench near the entrance. "Line up, two rows. Let's get warm. I catch you slacking and you're out."

"That's X," says Sunny in a whisper. "I think his real name is Xavier, but everyone just calls him X. He's the boss around here. I wouldn't cross him if I were you."

X takes them through a violent twenty minutes of sit-ups, push-ups, on-the-spot sprints and stretches. Jason is pleased to learn he's in good shape compared to most of the other trainees. There's a wiry kid who kicks his ass in the push-ups though. Jason makes a mental note to double his daily workout. There's jack shit to do at the group home anyway. He doesn't have a phone, there's only one computer in the place, and he doesn't care enough to fight for a spot in front of the TV. So Jason usually spends most evenings on his own in his room, trying to bulk up. Since he started hormone therapy, he's gotten way stronger, with bigger shoulders, a broader chest. His muscles are one of the only things he likes about his body. Muscles and the soft mustache that's beginning to fill in on his upper lip. Becca used to tease him about it, calling it a little caterpillar. Jason's proud though. He feels like he fought a *war* for the right to have this mustache.

As he pushes his body through a series of punches that X demonstrates for them, Jason zones out. He finds himself remembering his dad teaching him how to throw a punch. He was around six years old. His dad took Jason's small hand in his larger one and folded it into a fist. Talked him through the bits to hit. If you have to hit someone. If they make you. The places that will make them stop hitting you. Throat, eyes, solar plexus, nose. Stuff that crushes or breaks.

"Focus, kid." X kicks Jason on the side of the knee, opening his stance up a little more. Jason shakes his head, willing himself to just be here, in the moment.

Sweat drips in his eyes, stinging. It feels better than crying.

Chapter Four

"Jason, get in here." Ron, the care worker, leans his skinny body out of the office.

Shit.

"Got another call from the school today." Ron sits down in an old wooden chair as Jason walks into the office.

Even if he'd wanted to, Jason can't smile at Ron or try to come up with some charming excuse. Not when Ron has told him over and over that Becca died of an overdose. Told him that the police have looked into it and what they say must be right. Not when Ron has never once asked Jason why his nose was bloody or his shirt sleeve was ripped.

Ron tries, Jason knows. Ron has fourteen kids to look after. There's not enough money, time or space for any of them. Jason usually cuts him a lot of slack for missing the obvious.

"Yeah?" he manages not to add, *So what?*

"You're skipping." Ron sounds a thousand years old.

"Obviously," Jason replies. He places his hands on the wall behind him, digging his nails into the plaster.

"If you skip, you'll get suspended," Ron points out, like this isn't the fifteenth time they've had this conversation.

"Yeah. And then I won't have to go to school." Jason doesn't understand why they think this is a bad thing.

"You'll end up in an alternative school if you keep going this way."

Jason shrugs like he always does. What does it matter if they send him off to a school for losers and gang kids? He's not exactly going to get a shot college.

Ron sighs and rubs his big nose. "Group starts in ten. You be there." The *or else* hangs in the room for a minute. Jason's not sure what the punishment for missing it would be, but he doesn't want to change homes again. At least here he knows who to avoid and how to make sure they leave him alone. For the most part.

"Okay." He slips out of the room before Ron can say anything else.

The shower's being used, so Jason yanks off his T-shirt and wipes himself with it. He probably smells like sweat and old socks, but who cares? Group sucks, and Jason's not going to pretty himself up for it. He probably won't even talk. Yeah, that'll piss Ron off. If he doesn't even say anything. They can make his body be there, but they can't make him talk.

Cheered by the thought of annoying everyone with silence, he changes quickly. Then he runs down the stairs, leaving his sweaty kit on the floor of his room. The only reason he's got his own room is that if any of the other kids see him naked, his secret will be out. But the other kids think it's special treat-ment for no reason. It made them hate him right from the start.

Group is held in the living area. When Jason enters, Ron is fighting with one of the Owen twins over the Xbox control. The room is packed full of grouchy, moody teens.

Tash McAdam

Derek is on the single unbroken
armchair, while his crew fills out the
beat-up old couch. Two beanbags hold
five teens between them, sprawled out
and comfortable with each other.

Jason heads for the space between
the bookshelf and the corner of the room.
He leans against the wall, deliberately
choosing something to think about.
Winning the lottery, he decides. Finding
a scratcher on the street, unused. Not
too much money—don't get greedy.
Enough to start a life when he ages out.
Maybe a hundred grand. Yeah. That
sounds perfect.

It works for the first twenty minutes.
Ron asks everyone to share a good thing
that has happened to them this week.
Jason stays quiet, which gets a raised
eyebrow, but Ron doesn't press. Maybe
he understands that nothing good
happens to Jason anymore. Although
that's not strictly true.

If Ron had insisted, Jason would have said boxing. He could have said that he had a good time being in a space that smells like old sweat and shoes. That being in a place where everyone saw him as a man felt right. That beating up on an old bag, where the only thing he has to do is try, felt good.

After everyone except Jason has shared a good thing, Ron asks them to share a challenge. The usual "I did this hard piece of homework" or "I resisted the urge to" blah, blah and blah is boring. Jason completely zones out until he's surprised out of his thoughts by Derek's voice.

"I figured out who murdered Jason's slutty sister." Derek's stupid toad face spreads in an ugly grin. He's daring Jason to do something. Knowing he won't. Knowing that he's bigger, stronger and more dangerous than Jason. Everything Jason isn't.

To his own surprise, Jason discovers he doesn't care. Anger fills him, and suddenly he's twenty feet tall and made of rock. He's going to smash Derek's evil face in. He throws himself out of his corner, kicking off the wall. The force slams him into Derek, knocking him right out of the armchair. Jason lands on top of him.

Around him the group bursts out in yells. Hands grab him, trying to pull him away or push him forward. Under Jason's knees, Derek's big chest fills with air. Jason swings for his face like he's chopping wood, pow, pow, pow. His knuckles sting and split, but he can barely feel it. Then Derek's fist explodes into his side. He feels that.

He's thrown a few feet across the room, into the bookshelf. It shudders and drops a bunch of old paperbacks on top of him. Derek looms over him and lifts his leg. Jason tries to squirm away but gets a sneaker to the jaw. Pain bursts through his face, and his vision blurs.

Chapter Five

They have to drag Derek off Jason. It takes Ron plus two of the bigger boys. Jason's whole body is screaming from the kicking and stomping before they manage it.

Ron calls an ambulance, because Jason can't even sit up. His head feels like a rotten watermelon that's about to burst open.

It's not as bad as it could have been. Four stitches in his eyebrow, bruised ribs. Bruised *everywhere*. If Jason had been born with a dick, he'd probably have needed surgery. As it is, he just has a huge purple bruise spreading up the front of his thigh to his stomach. He doesn't tell the doctor he's injured there, barely even lets them look at his ribs. The pressure of eyes on him, seeing him as female, catching themselves on *his* pronouns. It all sucks worse than the pain. He gets some pretty good pills for it though. Ron holds on to them for him, which is just as well. They'll go missing from his room within hours if he tries to keep them there.

Healing sucks. Ron makes him go to school the next day. His head hurts so much he feels sick. Ron drives up to the gates and takes him into the office. They have a brief and awful meeting with his vice-principal. Then Jason gets to spend the rest of the day being stared at by kids in the corridor. The black eye is more a black half face, true. But really, do they need to look quite that much?

He's definitely too sore to exercise, but he walks over to the gym after school gets out anyway. Sunny, Preet and Lucky are all sitting on the raised concrete entrance, feet dangling over the edge.

"Ho, shit, man. What happened to your face?" Lucky says, clearly torn between impressed and disbelieving.

"Fight," Jason replies shortly.

Lucky slips down from the platform and approaches, wrinkling his face in wonder. "Whoa."

"Did you win?" Preet asks, staying put on the ledge even though Sunny drops down to join Lucky in looking at Jason's damage.

"What does it look like? Jeez, get off, dude." Jason ducks away from Sunny's attempt to move his chin to inspect the bruises more closely.

He can't see properly out of his left eye, so hands on his shirt warn him too late. Lucky is behind him, pulling his shirt up, looking for bruises. Panic chokes him. Jason reacts without thinking, flinging his elbow back. It connects hard, and there's a second thud a moment later.

Jason spins around, panting. His heart is pounding. He hates people touching him at the best of times. Right now, bruised and in pain? Shit.

Lucky's looking up at him from the ground with a dizzy, confused expression. "Why did you hit me? And why are you wearing a bra?"

Jason almost laughs. To his horror, tears sting his eyes instead. He tries to reply, to make up some lie about it being a bandage for his ribs. Instead a sob bursts out of him. Suddenly he's just outright crying. It hurts. It hurts his face and his chest and his bruised fists. He can barely see through the salty tears. A soft touch on his shoulder makes him flinch.

"It's okay." Sunny sounds calm and not at all embarrassed or angry that Jason is weeping, unable to stop. "It's not a bra, Lucky. It's a binder. Jase, it's okay, bro. Don't worry about it."

The simple acceptance in Sunny's voice makes Jason cry harder. The "bro" says Sunny knows but hasn't changed his mind about maybe being friends. The relief Jason feels makes his whole body shake. Sunny just pats him on the shoulder again and waits for him to stop.

"What…?" Lucky says, confused.

"Shut up, Lucky." Preet jumps down from the railing. "Let's blow off training, guys. Get some ice cream."

"Uncle Jay'll kill me," Sunny moans. Then he starts walking back toward the main street. Jason follows. Behind them, Jason can hear Preet hissing at Lucky. Lucky keeps trying to reply, but she talks right over him every time.

They end up in McDonald's, having milkshakes and fries. Lucky dips his fries *in* the ice cream, which grosses out Jason enough that he finally stops shaking. He starts to feel more like himself again.

"Our cousin's non-binary trans," Sunny informs them while Jason's got his mouth full and can't reply immediately. "My uncle kicked them out, but we still see them sometimes. We've met some of their friends. Their boyfriend is a trans guy. So, like, we get it. It's cool. You do you. No big."

No big. Jason laughs and accidentally snorts ice cream up his nose. It's freezing. And it feels like getting punched in the face all over again.

"Shit, that hurts so much, oh my god," he gasps.

Everyone at the table cracks up laughing. But it's not mean laughter. It's something bigger and warmer than that. Preet's jammed into the booth next to him, and she leans her knee against his. That's warm too. Warm and solid and real.

The last person to touch Jason in a way that wasn't violent was Becca. With Preet's knee pressed into his leg, watching Sunny stealing Lucky's fries, Jason forgets to be sad, or angry. Instead, he just is.

Chapter Six

It's three weeks before Jason's able to box again. He spends those afternoons—after attending school like a good little boy—on the benches, watching. Sometimes he teases the others in the group as they learn the basic stance and punches. They even get to actually face off against each other a bit.

Even without the training the others are getting right now, Jason thinks he's still the best fighter of the bunch. At least he doesn't have to pay while he's on the bench. He was able to get four hundred dollars using Becca's ATM card. It makes uncomfortable lumps in his shoes, but he doesn't know where else to keep it.

The only good thing about Jason being bruised to hell and back is that Derek got kicked out of the group home. Even though Jason started the fight, Derek got in trouble with his social worker, and now he's been bounced somewhere else.

When his bruises have healed, Jason can't wait to get back to the gym. Excited to be fighting today, he whistles as he ducks into the small changing room. He kicks his sneakers off. He shoves them into the bag with his water bottle and clean shirt.

"Yo, good to see you back, kid," X says as he pulls his shirt off, exposing a strong, hairless chest. He's covered in thick black tattoos. "We got a tournament coming up next month. Figured you might want to take a shot at the Fish division. That's the new trainees. Anyone who hasn't competed before."

"Uh, maybe," Jason replies, grabbing his bag and heading back to the gym. He always changes into gear he can box in before he comes to the gym. One black T-shirt looks much like the next, after all. He still feels uncomfortable being in the changing room with someone else.

"You should think about it," X calls after him. "You got quick fists and the temper for it." He sounds a bit like he's laughing.

Jason takes it easy, but he's still dripping sweat and aching by the time the hour is up. Near the end of the training session the more experienced boxers start coming in. They stand by the walls and stretch. They also yell tips and curses at the teenagers working on the bags or each other.

It's easy to notice that Jason gets more compliments than insults. By the time his group is let off the mats a ball of pride is sitting in his chest, glowing. Instead of going straight out the door, he goes into the office. Little Jay's in there, doing some paperwork. He grins at Jason when he enters.

"Big Jay," Little Jay says and points finger guns at Jason.

"I, uh, was wondering about the tournament thing," Jason says. "What do I have to do?"

Little Jay gives him a long look. "You're not hurting anymore?"

"Not really." This isn't exactly true. Especially his jaw. It's still bruised. The light blows and padded gloves today stung a lot more than they should have.

"All right. I'll let X know. See you tomorrow. Ice your face." He smirks.

Jason does ice his face. He ices it while he pulls Becca's boxes out from under his bed. Other people have obviously gone through them—the curse of not having locks on the door—but there is nothing missing. Jason has the contents memorized. And no one's bothered taking the book from where Jason left it, in plain view on his bedside table. Jason often has books, library books mostly. Not even Derek has ever stolen or trashed those.

The photo of the gym, carefully flattened, is on top. Jason takes it out and looks at it, as he does almost every night. Then he pulls out the clippings one by one. There are eighteen of them. Eighteen girls, the youngest fifteen years old, the oldest twenty-seven. All missing.

Never found. All of them last seen somewhere in East Van.

Jason has memorized their names too. But he goes back over them one more time. He wants to learn more. Tomorrow, in social studies, they have a block in the computer lab. For research. But Jason's not going to be working on his history project.

Chapter Seven

True to form, the social studies teacher, Mr. Murti, doesn't even check to make sure they're on task. Jason picks a computer in the front. It's near the teacher, which means no one else will sit next to him. The other students haven't figured out that the front is the safest spot. If Mr. Murti ever does get up to check on them, Jason's will be the *last* computer he passes on his way back to the desk. Plenty of time to switch browser windows.

Jason puts two Chrome windows next to each other. He pulls up a time line of global trans rights on one side. His history project is about human rights in the twenty-first century. He has enough info to convince anyone he's been doing research.

His other window is private, for his other research. He googles the name of each girl in turn and makes notes of any new information. Nothing jumps out at him, but you never know. In the cop shows they're always collecting as much information as possible. Some small thing could turn out to be the most important clue.

Only a few of the missing girls have any details about family left behind. Most are single, young, living on the fringe. The kind of girls whose disappearance wouldn't really be noticed. Like Becca.

Except Becca has Jason. And he misses her like he'd miss a leg. He can feel her leaning over his shoulder. Kissing the top of his head and telling him that just because he's her brother now doesn't mean he's not still the baby.

His eyes sting. Putting his memories of Becca away, Jason finishes up his notes and shuts down his computer.

The day drags by. Jason skips gym class, which he's been doing since third grade. Everyone has pretty much given up on trying to make him go. He eats his lunch, alone, on the mostly empty D-block corridor near the metal shops. Somehow he makes it through math without falling asleep.

By the time the last bell rings, Jason's irritated and on edge. He heads to Ray's Place early, even though drop-in doesn't start until four. He's there before Sunny, Preet or Lucky.

"Welcome back," says X. He looms in the doorway to the office, smirking. "Hear you changed your mind about the fight."

Jason shrugs and says, "Yeah. Thought I'd give it a shot."

"Where did you learn to fight?" X pulls Jason out onto the gym floor. Grabs the bag right out of Jason's hand. It takes effort for Jason to let the bag go, not to challenge X—he knows that would be a stupid idea. X throws the bag against the wall and it thuds onto a bench. Then he turns to Jason and squares off, raising his fists.

Jason does the same thing. They don't have gloves or helmets or gum shields. "Around," he replies to X's question, closing his guard up so his elbows are close to his body.

The truth is, his dad gave him his only training back when Jason first started getting pushed around in school for being weird. For insisting he was a boy despite all the kids who pulled his pants down trying to prove otherwise. And there were a lot of kids trying to pull his pants down. His dad, an ex-military man, taught him to stop them. So, yeah, Jason knows the basics and puts in the time to build good muscles. His dad always said he had the raw talent of a fighter. Quick reactions and the ability to shake off a fair amount of pain. The day he broke Marc Denman's nose was the first day his dad ever called him son. Jason grins at the memory—just a twitch of the lip.

X must see, though, because he laughs. "Think you can take me, do ya?" He's joking around, but there's challenge there as well.

"Give me a few years," Jason replies and then lifts his hand to catch X's gentle punch.

They mess around on the mats until the rest of the teens show up. X shows Jason a couple of tricks, some head bobs and a bit of footwork. It's easygoing, a warm-up. Jason's body feels right when he boxes. It fits somehow.

"Hey, go sign up for the tournament, since you're already warm. Sheet's on my desk." X claps Jason on the shoulder, making him stagger.

Little Jay's in the office, sitting at the desk and counting cash. Behind him the safe door is partially open.

"What do you want, dude?" Little Jay stops counting, frowning at Jason.

"Sign up." Jason spots the form on the desk and motions toward it. "Can I?"

Little Jay just hands him a pen. Jason moves around the desk so he can put his name down on the form. *Under 18s, rookie*, he assumes. Just as he finishes writing his name, something catches his eye inside the safe. A trans flag! He'd recognize that baby blue, soft pink and white anywhere. A swelling feeling of happiness fills his stomach, and he beams, turning to see if Little Jay has noticed that *he's* noticed. Maybe they got it for him?

And then it hits him like a ton of bricks. It's not just a trans flag. It's a sticker of a trans flag, stuck to a USB stick. A USB he recognizes because he watched Becca stick that flag onto it. Becca's USB. In this safe.

Jay's still counting money, mouthing out the numbers. Jason's heart is pounding in his ears. He feels hot all over, bright red and swollen. He's about to explode. The pen falls out of his numb fingers, hitting the concrete floor loudly.

Little Jay makes an annoyed noise, puts down the pile of bills and starts again from the top. He's not paying attention to Jason at all. Why would he? All the money's in front of him.

It's stupid, but Jason can't control himself. Slowly he reaches out, keeping an eye on Little Jay the whole time. Little Jay doesn't even look up, and Jason forces himself not to rush. Swift movement draws attention.

Finally the cold plastic is in his sticky hand. He almost bangs his wrist on the safe door when X yells, "Jason, hurry up!" He quickly shoves the USB into the front of his boxers, in with his packer. Hopefully it just looks like he's scratching his balls.

Chapter Eight

Jason is on edge for the whole training session. X gets frustrated with his lack of attention, how he's always a beat behind the rest of the group, and sends him off to do weights in the corner. It's a relief to sit down on the bench with the USB digging into his thigh. He knows that he hasn't dropped it on the floor.

He stays for the whole session, though every inch of his body is screaming at him to get out of there. To get home and see what is on Becca's USB. And why it was in X's safe.

It could be evidence, something connecting the gym to Becca's death, to the missing girls. Should he take it straight to the police? His heart sinks as he realizes he has no proof that the USB ever *was* in the safe.

The cops will just think he's making stuff up. That he can't admit his sister was an addict. At best they'll come and search the gym. Who knows if there's anything here at all? Maybe there's a good explanation for the USB being in the safe. Maybe Becca was working for the gym or dating X. It could be any number of things.

Frustrated, Jason spends too long doing curls. He keeps it up until his arms refuse to complete another lift.

Across the gym, X watches him with a curious expression, like he's trying to figure out what's going on. The rest of the group starts packing up. Jason returns his weights to the stand and scrapes his sweaty hair off his face.

"Later," he tells X on his way past, not even stopping by the changing room to say bye to his friends. He's barely spoken to them today. They must know something's up.

He's jumpy all the way home. The number 20 bus is packed with its usual crowd. Jason huddles near the doors so he doesn't have to go near the drunk men at the back. He knows he passes as male now, but he can't forget the years of confusion and abuse. He can never relax in public spaces.

As soon as he gets back to his group home, he realizes he doesn't have any way of looking at the USB. *Idiot.* There is an ancient desktop in the shared main room, but with no idea of what's on the USB, he can't risk checking it out while people are still awake. That means he will have to wait.

The hours drag by. He kills some time making dinner. He wolfs down the mac and cheese standing by the sink, then goes back to hide in his bedroom. For the next couple of hours, he paces up and down the room, running over his plan. He'll wait until, like, 2 a.m. and then sneak down to the living room. Lift the desktop screen off the table. Turn it so he can hide next to the sofa with a blanket over his head to hide the light. Hopefully, no one will even notice he's out of bed.

He doesn't sleep, too scared he won't wake up. As soon as the old clock on his wall clicks to *2*, he slides out of bed. He's tense and sweaty as he tiptoes to the door and slowly pushes it open. Even though they'll just tell him to get his ass back to bed if he gets caught, he's scared.

The trip down to the living room goes okay until a loud groan breaks the silence. The creaky stair! It sounded awful, but now all Jason can hear is his own heartbeat.

He freezes on the stairs for a few minutes. His muscles are trembling from holding so still. No doors open, so he hurries the rest of the way down to the lounge.

Flattening himself against the wall, he waits to see if he's been discovered. It's quiet, and finally Jason forces himself away from the wall.

The computer always makes a sound when it boots up. So Jason carefully unplugs the speakers and gets under a blanket before pressing the power button. It takes forever to load. Jason reaches out from under the blanket and feels around on the desk.

He's trying to find the port to plug in the USB.

A throat clears. It's so loud Jason jumps and hits his chin on the monitor in his lap. The USB falls on the floor somewhere. He pulls the blanket off his head to see who's caught him. Ron is standing in the doorway, looking at him with a disappointed expression on his droopy, sad face. He's wearing flannel pajamas and looks ridiculous. Jason doesn't laugh.

"Buddy." The tired annoyance in Ron's voice makes Jason clench his jaw. He curls his hand tightly around the USB stick he managed to scoop up.

"Homework," Jason says, smiling at Ron. "It's due tomorrow, and I forgot."

"I want to believe you, Jason, but the last time you handed in a piece of home-work was months ago," Ron replies.

Words won't come. There are none in his head. He sits like a lump, shoulders hunched in. Just waiting to see what Ron will decide to do.

"Give me that." Ron moves closer, pointing at Jason's clenched fist.

The protest dies in his throat when he sees Ron's face. Ron doesn't do "don't push me" very often. When he does, he means it. Jason glares at his feet, cursing the hot tears that sting his eyes. It feels like all he does lately is cry. He cries at the stupidest times, when he least wants to. It's so hard to hand over the USB. The peeling sticker clings to his palm when Ron takes it from him. A tiny corner of blue sticks to his thumb. Ron puts the USB in his pajama pocket.

"I'm not going to look at this, and you can have it back when you prove to me that you can be trusted," Ron says. "We have rules here for a reason." He doesn't make a habit of taking things— unless they're illegal—from the kids in the house, so he must have really had it with Jason.

"I don't know how to make you start taking your life seriously, Jason. But if you don't... it's all downhill from here." Ron walks out of the room. He doesn't even wait to make sure Jason goes back to bed.

Chapter Nine

Three weeks pass. Jason is on his best behavior. He's been going to school, doing his homework *and* putting in hours every day at the gym. Soon the night of the tournament arrives.

Sunny is also competing in the beginners match, much to his uncle's delight. Little Jay has been bragging around the place that Sunny's going to take it, regardless of who shows up from the other local gyms. But Jason has heard X saying the smart money's on Jason.

That simple statement made Jason feel amazing. And X wasn't even saying it for Jason's benefit. He meant it.

Jason warms up with Sunny. They stretch together and then spar lightly. X yells tips at them both. Maybe Jason shouldn't be looking forward to beating his friend quite so much, but it's all in good fun.

"Boys, get in here and sign the waiver," Little Jay yells from the office. Jason and Sunny jog over, teasing each other. Jason ducks into the washroom on the way.

When he gets to the office, he sees a man he doesn't recognize. Little Jay waves a hand at him. "Big Jay, give the dude your ID and sign the thing, then get back out there."

Jason goes cold. He's stuck on Little Jay's words. *Give them your ID.* Jason's ID still has his birth name and his F gender marker.

Sunny shoulders him, gives him a look. "You okay, bro?" He raises an eyebrow.

Jason wipes his face and then nods. "Yeah. Yeah, I'm okay."

So what? So what if this dude finds out he's trans? Maybe he won't even notice or care. The contest is mixed genders, apparently. Jason hasn't seen any obviously female names on the sheet. Preet would have entered if she could, he knows. If she was allowed. And she's a better fighter than Sunny, maybe even Jason, from what he has seen.

Jason pulls his wallet out of his back pocket. He keeps it on him whenever he can. Old foster-care habits die hard.

The card feels wet in his hand. He puts it down on the desk.

"Sign here," the man says, pushing a sheet of paper at him. Jason quickly scribbles on the line. The dude doesn't even look up at him as he looks at the ID card. He takes the paper back from Jason. "Good luck." His words are neutral, no feeling or emotion. He's just a man doing a boring job. Jason breathes out in relief and grabs his card. He almost runs back out to the gym.

The ring looks cleaner than usual. There's a lot of people in the room. Jason recognizes only a couple of others from the training sessions. He guesses that people from other classes are here as well. The beginners' matches are first, but there's time to kill. While Jason stretches a bit more, he does some people watching.

Little Jay comes out, carrying a large chalkboard. He hangs it from hooks on the bare brick wall. He looks at the sheet of paper in his hand and starts writing stuff on the board.

Jason leans down to stretch his hamstrings and tries to focus on his body. His binder feels too tight. But he knows it fits him perfectly. The first time he wore a binder that actually fit, it was incredible. Instead of strapping down his chest with plastic wrap or even duct tape over a T-shirt, he had something proper. He had spent two uncomfortable years wanting to die every time he felt his chest move under his shirt. Being able to exercise comfortably was amazing. But now suddenly it feels like the binder doesn't fit at all. Like it's choking him.

"Yo, Big Jay. You chicken out?" X always manages to have a mocking note in his voice, but this is straight-up aggressive.

Jason twitches upright like he's been stung. "No, I just signed in."

"They must have fucked it up then"—X slings his arm over Jason's shoulder—"because some girl's up first."

Jason's throat closes. He wants to run away and rip his shirt from his body, but his feet are glued to the floor. He looks at the chalkboard.

He swallows and tries to speak, but it doesn't work. The words stick in his throat. X gives him a weird look. Jason swallows again, clears his throat. "That's…uh…that's me. Jane Ross. My…my old name."

Is X going to throw him out now that he knows he's trans? Will he kick his ass? Jason waits, unable to move. His whole body is made of fresh cement, wet and thick and heavy.

"*Jane…Ross.*" X holds the words in his mouth like he's tasting them. "Huh."

X lifts his hand away from Jason's

back and settles it on his neck. Squeezes. The strength there is iron—no way to escape.

"Go get 'em, *Jason*." He smirks and pushes Jason in the direction of the ring. Jason stumbles forward. His legs feel like they belong to someone else.

Ducking under the rope, Jason has never felt so awkward and out of place. X's eyes are drilling holes into the back of his neck. He wonders what X is seeing. Is he noting the curve of Jason's hips, the sway he can't quite erase when he walks?

He shakes his head and tries to focus. His opponent is in the opposite corner. A heavily muscled dude in a grubby tank top is yelling in his face. The kid looks to be around Jason's real age, seventeen, a beard just coming in on his cheeks. He has the wide sort of face the best fighters tend to have. Flat bones that are hard to split the skin on.

Suddenly Jason needs to pee. It makes no sense because he went, like, ten minutes ago. His body tries to insist, but Little Jay hustles him into his corner before he can make a "be right back" face and run off. It's probably for the best. Jason's not sure he would have the nerve to come back.

"You got this, kid," Little Jay tells him. He shakes Jason by the shoulders and hands him his kit. Jason puts in his gum shield, relieved he doesn't have to talk. The taste of plastic fills his mouth, and he bites down hard. Little Jay nods and helps him with his helmet. Then he hands Jason his gloves to pull over his hand wraps.

Little Jay bops him on the head and ducks out of the ring. The ref is checking Jason's opponent's gear.

When the ref comes over to his corner, Jason feels his nerves drop away. Something in his blood is rising. There's a small crowd gathering around the ropes, cheering already. Jason is surprised to see how many people are present, since these are considered the baby matches, the warm-ups.

The ref nods and waves him into the center. Jason's opponent skips forward, hands in the air like a champion. He's working the crowd up. Jason stands still, his body settling. He feels his muscles relaxing, coolness pouring through him like water.

He's ready.

Chapter Ten

Apart from flat cheekbones, the other guy doesn't have much going for him. Jason runs rings around him. He has quicker reactions and a better guard. In fact, his opponent barely lays a glove on him.

Jason is declared the winner of each of the three bouts. Usually boxing matches go way longer than that, but the juniors just get in for three rounds. He's not even bruised. He saunters out of the ring feeling like he's walking on air.

He has two more matches, but Sunny's up first. His opponent is already gloved and ready on the mats. The guy—his name is Jack, according to the board—is a stocky sort of dude with heavy shoulders and a square jaw. He looks tough. Indeed, Sunny only wins one of the three matches. And he has bruised ribs and a split lip to show for it.

Then Jason's back in. There's another new competitor facing off in the blue corner. The gloves feel good on Jason's hands. The whoops of the crowd are in his blood. He's pumped.

It's a closer match, but Jason takes it two to one. He ends up with a swollen eyebrow. It's the only bill he has to pay for his second win of the night.

As the loser preps to take on the winner of Sunny's round, Jason checks the board. He's relieved to see that someone has rubbed some letters off his name so it just reads *J. Ross*. Then he realizes with a jolt that he's listed in the finals. Up for silver or gold! If Jack wins, Jason will have to fight him, but if the guy he just fought takes this match, Jason has won the whole thing already with only two fights. This could be it!

He joins Sunny, Lucky and Preet by the ropes. He groans along with them as Jack pummels the other guy for an easy three–nothing win.

"Well," Sunny says with a smirk, "at least I lost to the winner. Uncle Jay can't be too pissed about that."

"Can't he?" Preet snickers and then pokes Jason in the shoulder. "Stay warm, loser, you're about to get called."

Jason grins at her. His face feels like it's cracking open. "About to get silver, more like." He's puffing his chest out, tall and strong. He feels so good right now with bruises slowly flowering on his face. Like he could fight a giant.

And he's about to, he realizes as he gets in the ring. Sunny is a pretty tall guy, so all Jason had registered was that Jack was shorter than Sunny. But he's got a few inches on Jason, and he's built like a truck. They touch gloves. The ref waves them apart and then flags the start.

Jason skips forward, light on his feet. He doesn't want to give Jack the offensive immediately. After watching him pummel his last opponent, Jason has a healthy respect for the force Jack can put behind his gloves. But Jason thinks he's faster.

He moves in on fast feet. He ducks his left shoulder in to cover his front and then twists his body to throw a mid-range punch. He's planning to follow up with a hook from his left.

Instead, somehow, he finds himself staring at the ceiling of the gym. His whole face hurts. The ref leans into his vision, and Jason's hearing suddenly restarts. "Three, four..." The ref is counting! He has to get up.

The world lurches a little as Jason moves and then steadies. He gets to his feet. He presses his thick gloved hand to his jaw. The sense of general pain has settled into a screaming ache right on the base of his jaw. Second time in two months—yikes. He can taste blood in his mouth. He retreats gratefully to his corner.

He rinses his mouth and wipes his face with a towel. He heads back into the ring, ignoring Little Jay completely.

Jack lines up to face him, they tap, and it's on again. Jason's head is still a little foggy. He closes his guard up and settles himself down into his shoulders, keeping it tight and close. He takes a bunch of blows to the arms, but nothing the muscles there can't absorb. And he gets in a few hits of his own on Jack's sides as the two of them close up and pull apart.

The crowd yells as the boxers trade blows. Jason's distracted, trying to protect his face. If he suffers another punch in the jaw, he's down for good. He takes a couple of hard hits to the ribs but pushes through them. Adrenaline keeps the pain down for now. And then he sees it, an opening. When Jack swings forward for a big right hook, there's a gap under his defensive elbow.

Jason's not quick enough, but he blocks the flurry of blows and waits. There. Jack pushes forward too far, up on his toes. Jason sways away from the glove and drives his fist right into Jack's side. The impact crushes his glove.

The air whooshes out of Jack's lungs. He staggers, dropping his guard just an inch. It's enough.

Jason puts his whole body into one more punch. It starts in his feet and swings through his whole body. His glove slams into Jack's jaw. He actually watches Jack's eyes glaze over.

Jack slams to his knees and then to his side. The ref counts it, but Jason already knows. He's won.

Chapter Eleven

He floats on his victory for the whole
evening. It's fun watching the rest of the
matches. Afterward Sunny takes them all
for donuts and hot chocolate. He doesn't
seem upset that he lost his fight. Jason
doesn't even miss his curfew. But he could
have stayed out all night, he's so happy.

The next day he's still walking on
air. He has a black eye—again—and a

bruised jaw. They're the first injuries he's ever felt good about. In the mirror he admires the purple bump on his eyebrow. He earned that bruise, decided to fight a battle and won. The marks feel like medals.

He didn't get a trophy for the tournament. But the smiles and cheers were reward enough. He'll have the memory of that forever. A moment when everyone around him saw him, Jason. They were on his side.

Walking to the gym after school, he's almost bouncing down the street. The air is cold, but the sun is high in the sky. Even the Downtown Eastside seems brighter than usual.

Little Jay is outside the gym, talking on his phone. When he sees Jason he gives him a wide grin and holds out his fist for a bump. Jason heads in, still buzzing. People call out greetings to him in a way they've never done before.

He gets more high fives and bumps on the way to the changing room.

He feels like he's glowing. There's a warm ball inside his chest. For months he's felt like there's ice inside him. Only ice, cold and hard and solid. Today the ice has melted. Jason feels as though he's alive again. He can feel things that aren't pain and sadness and loss.

The men's changing room has four or five people in it, as always. Jason turns his back to them to pull his sweats off, stuffing them into his bag. He'll have to get shoes for boxing, if he wants to keep it up. Barefoot's okay for now, but most of the others wear special shoes. Maybe Ron will help him figure out how to pay for them, since he's doing so much better now. Staying in school and getting his work done and everything.

Jason feels something hard prodding him in the back. He turns, laughing. He expects to see someone else wanting to congratulate him. Or maybe Sunny messing around. But it's X. Standing there with both hands in his hoodie pockets.

"What's up, man?" Jason asks, grinning.

"Where's the USB, Jason Ross?" X demands sternly.

Jason's stomach lurches.

X moves his hand, still inside the pocket of his hoodie. There's something in X's pocket, a familiar hard shape. And it's pointed straight at Jason. He remembers the poke to his back, sees the cold look in X's eyes. Terror washes over him.

The USB. X must have realized it is missing and somehow figured out that Jason took it. But how? It only takes him a moment to figure it out.

Becca Ross. Jason Ross. Not an unusual surname by any means. But a link to a missing USB. A USB with a trans flag on it even. Not so hard to put together.

X jerks his chin, moves his hand. His hand with what looks like a gun in it. "Spill, Jason. Where is it?"

There are still three other people in the changing room. X wouldn't shoot him here, surely, in front of everyone. It would be loud and messy. And even if they kept X's secret, there are two dozen more people out in the gym. A gunshot would be noticed.

And then Jason realizes what it all means. If X is this angry about a missing USB, it must mean he killed Becca. Or knows who did.

Jason shifts his weight onto his back foot. X shifts his own, clearly expecting a punch. But when Jason was younger, he played soccer. Although his dribbling was awful, he was great at penalty kicks.

X narrows his eyes at Jason like he's daring him. A split second later he realizes his mistake. Jason's sneaker-clad foot flies up. It connects with X's groin so hard it makes Jason's teeth snap shut. X makes a gasping, airless noise and folds to the floor.

Jason's already moving. He leaps over X's puking body and runs for the door. Hands reach out to stop him. The people who were clapping him on the back moments ago try to grab him, but Jason runs.

Chapter Twelve

He runs right through the gym and out the door. Hops the metal barrier like he can do parkour or something. He sees Sunny's surprised face. He barrels past the entrance to the alley, hangs a left and sprints for the main road. He hears shouts behind him. He doesn't know if X is up and chasing him or if others are. He doesn't have time to stop and look.

Ahead of him he sees the number 20 bus pulling in to a stop. Jason finds a burst of energy made by anger and desperation.

The bus is closing its doors. Jason skids to a halt next to it and slams his hand against the glass panel. Behind him footsteps pound the pavement. The yells get closer. He chances a look. It's Little Jay and two other big guys from the gym. They're blasting people out of their way on the busy sidewalk.

A hiss brings his attention back to the bus. To his relief the doors jerk open again. He slips between them. The bus pulls away, leaving the men shaking their fists at Jason through the window.

Heart pounding, he taps his transit card and slips into a seat.

Where should he go? If he goes back to the group home, they'll find him. They have his address, after all. And if X killed Becca, if he *killed Becca...*

Jason's vision grays out. In his head he sees Becca being held down while someone injects drugs into her arm.

A whining sound fills the air. For a few moments he doesn't realize it's coming from him. Blinking away tears, he glances around. People have moved away from him, except for the giggling meth heads. No one will meet his eyes.

He imagines what he must look like, sweaty from running, with all his bruises from last night.

The bus pulls in to a stop, and Jason leaps up and flies out the door. He almost knocks some guy off a scooter on the sidewalk.

"Jason!" The yell makes him whirl around, hands up.

Sunny is waving at him from a yellow cab. "Jason, get *in*," Sunny says.

Jason looks frantically from side to side, expecting X and his thugs to roll up at any second.

"It's just us! Let's go!" Preet screams as she climbs out of the other side of the taxi. She runs across the road toward Jason, almost getting hit by a car for her trouble.

She grabs him by the arm and yanks him back across the road. Her fingers are tight like iron. Jason's brain feels slow and stupid. He stumbles as she packs him into the taxi. Lucky turns around and makes a "WTF?" face from the front seat.

Sunny hands Jason the seat belt. Preet slams the door behind her, almost sitting on Jason's lap. The taxi driver finds Jason's eyes in the mirror.

"Where to?" he asks calmly, like nothing weird is going on at all.

"VCC Clark," Lucky says as he slides down in his seat, pulling his ball cap lower. "Let's go."

Every time Jason starts to talk, Preet pinches his thigh. Not in a kind way.

Her fingers are strong and hard. He's definitely going to have a bunch of little round bruises. He wants to ask, "What are you doing here?" and "What happened at the gym after I ran out?" and "How did you find me?" But she won't let him talk. He doesn't dare ask the worst question—"Are you taking me to X?"

Ten minutes of driving and as many painful pinches later, they pile out of the taxi at the SkyTrain station. Finally Jason is allowed to speak. "Why are we...here?" he asks nervously.

"It's a good hiding spot," Lucky replies calmly. He starts walking up a hill, away from the transit entrance. "C'mon. You have some explaining to do."

They walk in silence, and Lucky leads the way through some old, worn fencing. They have to drop down off a wall into a little stand of trees.

From here you can't see the road at all. Broken glass and old tarps hint that it's a refuge for the homeless.

"I used to crash here when home got too bad." Lucky says. He leads them through a small, almost hidden path, and suddenly they're in a little clearing. Lucky leans against a tree and then points at Jason.

"So what the fuck is going on?"

Chapter Thirteen

Jason doesn't know where to start. So he blurts out the biggest thing. The thing so big he can't even really believe it's true. "I think X killed my sister."

"Dude, what?" The disbelief in Lucky's voice comes through loud and clear. "Why the fuck would X kill your sister? I didn't even know you had a sister."

"Had. Yeah. She died before I met you." Jason crumples into a ball, resting his back against a fallen log. The whole story comes spilling out. The supposed overdose. The fact that Jason's dad died of an overdose. That Becca would never in a million years have touched a needle. The box of clippings in her room. All the missing girls, going back years. The USB stick. The gun in X's pocket.

When he's done puking up words, everyone just stares at him with blank, shocked faces. Jason is out of steam though. He can't fill the silence anymore. So he just waits.

"You...kicked...X...in the nuts?" Lucky asks in a strangled voice after a few minutes of heavy silence.

Preet shoves Lucky. "That's what you take from this? Not the fact that Jason's living a bad movie of the week?

That we might be getting taught to box by a murderer?"

Lucky looks a little embarrassed. "Sure, but like...that's wild. He kicked X in the nuts! *X!* He's lucky he's still alive." There's a pause, and Lucky pulls a face. "I mean, not because X is maybe a killer, but because, bro...he's a maniac, you know."

"Well, what are we going to do now?" Sunny asks.

We. He said *we.* And just like that, Jason is no longer alone. People know his secret, and they want to help. Tears sting his eyes, but he manages not to let them fall. Preet punches him in the shoulder in a friendly kind of way. Jason gives her a weak smile.

"I don't know," he replies. "X knows where I live. It's on my forms."

"So you can't go home," Sunny says. "Because, like, bringing a gun to the gym to threaten you with makes X look pretty fucking guilty if you ask me."

Lucky nods in agreement, but Preet looks skeptical. "What if it wasn't a gun?" she asks. "That's a hell of a power move. He's not going to shoot Jason in the gym, is he? It's more likely he was just trying to scare him. Find out what he knows."

"Well, it worked," Jason says. "The scare part, I mean. I don't know anything. My group-home leader, Ron, has the USB stick, so if there's evidence on there, I don't know what it is. Besides, the police wouldn't listen to me before, so why they would now?"

"So it sounds like there's two options," Preet says. "Catch X doing something suspicious enough that the police would *have* to pay attention. Or steal the USB stick and hope there's something really obvious on it."

"*And* hope the police believe I took it from X," Jason adds.

"Yeah."

"You know," Sunny says slowly, "Uncle Jay always covers the Friday-night shift because X has 'business.' "

"It's Friday tomorrow," Preet says. "What if we follow X, see what kind of *business* he's into?"

"You guys would do that for me?" Jason asks, shocked and touched.

Preet shrugs. "If it's between helping you out or learning you've died in mysterious circumstances, I'd rather try to help. Less guilt that way."

Lucky grins. "I always wanted to be a spy!"

It's a rough night. The others take off for a bit, but Jason stays where he is. It's too risky to be out in the open. Later Sunny and Preet bring him dinner, a shitty little tent that barely stays up and a couple of blankets. The ground is cold and uncomfortable. Every little noise jolts Jason awake and scares the crap out of him. Eventually he drifts off into an uneasy doze.

In the morning the rustle of nylon wakes him. He sits upright, his heart pounding. His fists swinging wildly, he manages to bring the tent down on top of him. It takes a minute to wriggle free of the fabric. When he emerges, he finds Lucky laughing his ass off, sitting on a tarp. The air is cold. Jason brings his blanket with him as he crawls out into the dawn light.

"Brought you breakfast." Lucky holds up a McDonald's bag. "Figured you'd be skipping class, so I also brought a book."

Jason laughs when Lucky taps the cover of *Us Weekly* on the tarp next to him. "Thanks, I think." He takes the brown bag from Lucky and practically inhales the food. There's coffee too, he realizes. He grabs it and scalds his mouth getting it down. Lucky laughs again and punches him on the shoulder.

"Don't just jerk it all day. Preet's going to bring you lunch. Then we'll come pick you up for Operation What the Fuck." Lucky hands Jason a bag he hadn't noticed before. "Here. Supplies."

With that Lucky gets to his feet and stretches. "I have to get my ass to school," he says. "We can't all sit around all day like losers. See ya!" He holds his fist out.

Jason taps it. "Thanks, Lucky. Catch ya later."

Lucky salutes him and picks his way back to the fence through the trees.

In the bag there's an actual book. It's an old sci-fi paperback. There's also a couple of bottles of water, a pair of boxer shorts, some toilet paper and a

Mars bar. Jason eats the Mars bar right away. He regrets it almost immediately. That was going to be the highlight of a boring, jumpy day.

Chapter Fourteen

In Jason's sweaty hand, the phone Preet
lent him buzzes as a text comes in.

LUCKY: **Got him. Odlum and
Parker. Right on time.**

Jason texts back quickly.

JASON: **OMW!**

Sunny sends a thumbs-up in return.
Jason jogs down the street. The plan is
to cover all the different directions X

could head after leaving his apartment. They don't want to lurk right outside, because there is nowhere good there to wait. It would have been really obvious. As it is, Jason's been chilling in Mosaic Park for a good two hours. His butt is cold and stiff from sitting on the stones for so long. Hood up, he ducks into an alley and waits for Lucky to update him.

LUCKY: **Heading toward Hastings, Sunny**

SUNNY: **Stay with him**

PREET: **I see him**

Jason heads up a block so he's not on the same street as X and waits for another update. The moon is covered by thick, misty-looking clouds. The few streetlights are the only thing lighting up the roads. For anyone else, it would be creepy, but Jason was raised in this 'hood.

PREET: **He's heading for the park**

Jason speeds up a bit. Then he sprints north on Woodland and races past the high school. He doesn't stop until he's almost across the parking lot. On the other side of the main road he makes out a figure just before it disappears, heading toward the large park—and Jason's favorite ice cream place.

PREET: **Where r u?**

LUCKY: **Lapped you. I'm at the park**

JASON **Almost there**

He sprints across the road as soon as the light changes. Then he presses himself up against the wall so he can peek around the corner. He's scared that X will have somehow heard him over the traffic. The road is clear, though, so he carefully walks on. The man he thinks is X stays a block ahead of him. A cat bursts out of a bush. Jason jumps and only just manages to swallow his scream. The trees appear out of the darkness, big and pointed like witches' hats.

The streetlights seem far away here. There's no light spilling over the spiky grass of the large park.

LUCKY: **I'm in the bushes in the middle**

Jason knows this park, even though it's too dark to make anything out. He knows there are two big squares of grass. Between them are a bathroom, a small play area and an empty swimming pool surrounded by bushes. If Lucky's in the middle, he'll have a view of either side, even in the dark. But unless they get close, they're not going to be able to hear anything.

X steps off the road and onto the grass, takes a couple of big strides up the hill and then sits down on an old bench. Jason can't see anyone else right now, can't figure out what X is doing. Maybe he's just out for a walk. Maybe all his business gets taken care of at his place. He could be about to go for ice cream even.

A shape detaches itself from the darkness in the middle of the park. For a wild second Jason thinks it's Lucky coming over, but the shadow is too big. It's a large man, definitely not a skinny teenager.

Jason inches closer, using the parked cars for cover. He makes his way down the road until he's hiding behind a camper van just two parked cars away from X.

"What are you doing?" X's voice is so low that Jason has to strain to hear.

Jason points his phone in their direction. On the screen they are just dark shapes, but maybe the phone will pick up sound.

"Taking a piss," the other man says, laughing quietly. The man heads for a parked car and pops the trunk. It's facing away from Jason, so he can't see inside. "Good enough?" the man asks X.

"Yeah, it'll do." X rustles in his jacket pocket, and the material moves enough that Jason sees the gun under X's arm.

Jason's stomach clenches. He suddenly realizes how stupid this is. Following a guy you think is a murderer?

X pulls out a big envelope. He hands it to the guy and gets some car keys in exchange.

A yell splits the night. Jason jumps but manages to keep his cover. He presses his body up against the cool metal of the camper van. He tries to peer through the darkness and see what's happening.

X slams the trunk and pushes the big guy. "Go see what's going on," X tells him.

The dude turns and runs off into the shadows of the park. Jason watches, his heart in his throat. There are a few soft noises, and then the man drags something out of the bushes.

It's Lucky, struggling to escape. "Get off me!" he yells, his voice thin and high with panic.

Jason freezes. He doesn't know what to do. His fingers are numb and clumsy as he holds the phone, pointing it at Lucky and the man who grabbed him. The only thing he can think to do is keep recording.

Lucky gets dragged, kicking and wriggling, across the park. The man tosses him at the car. He lands with a heavy thud. "It's just a kid."

"I know this kid," X growls, looking angry and wild. He scrubs his hand over his bald head, which is gleaming in the low light. "And if he's here, there's probably more of them. Shit."

Lucky tries to make a break for it. He slides down the trunk of the car, but he's grabbed before he can escape. X stands over him. Even from twenty feet away Jason can see that X's face is twisted in anger. "You brats teaming up with that little shit Jason? Why can't you fuckin' assholes just stay out of my business?"

"Did you kill Jason's sister?" Lucky almost screams it. Jason wonders if any of the people asleep in the houses around here are going to wake up.

X sighs, picks up Lucky by the front of his shirt and punches him in the face.

Jason pushes off from the van he's behind without a thought in his head. "Leave him alone!" he screams, sprinting toward X. He has no plan, but he can't just watch X beat up Lucky.

Too late, he realizes that's probably exactly why X hit Lucky. X drops Lucky, who crumbles in a heap on the ground. Then X turns to face Jason, pulling his jacket back to show his gun.

"What's your plan here, Jason?" X asks, sounding almost reasonable.

But Jason can see the edge of rage in his eyes. Hear it in his voice. "What's *your* plan?" he yells back, skidding to a halt. He's just out of X's reach. Behind X, the big man shifts forward. "Are you going to kill us?"

"Yeah, are you going to kill us?" A voice behind Jason makes him jump. He glances back as quickly as he can, not wanting to take his eyes off X. Preet and Sunny are shoulder to shoulder, both of them holding their phones up in front of them.

"Cause I'm livestreaming," Preet adds. "And I already called the police. You just punched a teenage boy in the face."

Lucky groans from the ground, muttering something that sounds like "Yeah, fuck you."

X looks from Preet to Sunny. He looks at Lucky on the ground and Jason standing in front of him, trembling with anger.

Jason hears sirens. Blue and red lights glint at the corner of the park and race toward them.

X runs. The man with him swears and sprints after him, disappearing into the darkness.

By the time the police cars pull up, Jason's helping Lucky to his feet, inspecting the damage.

"Do I look tough?" Lucky slurs through a split lip.

"Super tough," Jason tells him, almost laughing. Preet and Sunny talk to the police, and soon after that a police car heads off, sirens wailing.

"What's this about a USB stick, son?" a friendly police officer asks Jason, leading him away from Sunny.

And Jason tells them everything.

The cops call Ron to pick Jason up and give him a general overview of what just happened. All the way home, Ron alternates between *I can't believe you'd be so stupid* and *I'm sorry I didn't listen to you, Jason.* The cop who follows them back to the care home takes the USB from Ron with gloved hands, promising to keep them posted.

Jason drifts between the group home and school. He goes nowhere and talks to nobody, even when Ron tells him Sunny and Preet are outside.

He just waits.

He dreams of X pulling back his jacket, aiming the gun at him. X presses the gun between his eyes. Jason always wakes up then, gasping.

The day the cops come back to talk to him is the three-month anniversary of Becca's death. It's only been two weeks of waiting. But the days have blurred so much that it may as well have been a year.

He just sits quietly while they tell him where things are at. Two days earlier,

X was arrested on charges of assault. The USB that Jason stole and Ron took from him has X's fingerprints on it. It also contains spreadsheets that appear to pertain to a large-scale human-trafficking operation. The police also tell Jason that X co-owns a bar that both the missing girl and Becca worked at. They seem to think it will all be straightforward from here. They just have to prove X was involved with or was running this ring and Becca caught on. X must have killed her, or had her killed because of her snooping around. Now that the police believe Becca wasn't just another junkie, they're a lot nicer to talk to.

Jason gets a serious lecture about letting the police do their jobs and about getting involved with dangerous situations, but that's all. Slowly a weight lifts off his shoulders. It's done. They believe him. Becca's not going to be remembered as a dead addict.

After they leave, he borrows Ron's phone.

"Hey, it's Jason."

"Jason!" Sunny answers. "It's Jason, everybody!" he yells.

Jason smiles.

Chapter Fifteen

Jason looks around the room that's been his home for the last three years. He's pretty sure he's got everything. He didn't have much to start with. A few pictures, some beat-up books, his clothes—all from Value Village at this point. His binders are the only precious things he owns.

The day he'd been dropped here, he was fourteen. He was empty-handed, exhausted and emotional. An orphan. The plan since then had always been the same—wait it out until he wasn't a ward of the state anymore and then go to Becca. Becca hadn't been able to get custody. She'd been too poor, she worked nights, and she didn't have enough room. It was only a few years though. It was going to be okay. She'd save up, Jason would try to finish high school. Then he'd move in with her. Sleep on the sofa until they could afford to get a two-bedroom place. Them against the world.

With Becca dead, Jason's only plan had fallen apart. He had spent months trying not to imagine this moment, but now it's here. Time to move out, move on. Another kid needs the room. Probably more than one kid, since most of the rooms have at least two occupants. Jason's leaving means two more kids will have a bed. He's an adult now. Eighteen. On his own.

Jason's leaving means everything's changed.

He grabs his duffel bag and swings it over his broad shoulder. He's packed on even more muscle since he started boxing. The weight benches really helped him bulk out. He's getting a bit of a triangular shape now. It makes him look more like a young adult than a teen. His reflection in the grime-covered mirror catches his attention. Hollow-eyed, sure. Tired—always. But he's standing up straight. There's a confidence in the way he's holding himself—pride even? He doesn't hate his reflection, and that's something. Something big. He grins at himself and then turns his back on the empty gray room.

Ron is in the office, sorting through paperwork, when Jason thuds down the stairs.

"Ready to go, buddy?" Ron asks, glancing up through the little window.

"Yeah." Jason nods and then repeats himself with more certainty. "Yes. I'm ready."

Ron watches him for a moment and then smiles, his usually sad face brightening up. "You know what? I think you are."

Jason rolls his eyes. But the words settle in his chest in a warm heap. Ron's not so bad. To avoid any more feelings, Jason heads out to the car. Ron drives a beat-up old Jetta. Jason leans on the hood. The summer sunshine feels good on his bare arms.

"All right, let's hit it. You got the address?" Ron asks.

"Right here," Jason says, hunting in

his pocket for the scrap of paper. "We're headed to 627 Semlin."

"Sticking to the East. Smart boy." Ron leans across the front seat to let Jason in.

Jason climbs in, pushing his bag over into the back.

"Got lucky, I guess," Jason says as he winds down the window, letting a breeze into the small and kind of stinky car.

Ron starts the car and spins them out onto the road. "You deserve a little luck, Jason."

The rest of the ride passes in silence, Jason looking out the window at the passing houses and cars. It's his 'hood, his locals.

Ron parks right in front of the address Jason gave him and waits for Jason to open his door. It takes Jason a minute. A few minutes. Everything is changing—again. He's been through so much change, none of it good, over the *years*. He can't shake the feeling that this is going to be bad too. No matter what, it won't be Becca opening the door for him.

He grits his teeth and hops out of the car. Ron leans out the open window. "Want me to come up?"

Jason shakes his head. What's Ron going to do? Either try to big it up or bring it down. Jason's eighteen now. He can do it by himself. His stomach lurches.

"Uh, could you wait?" he asks, the words almost getting stuck in his throat. "In case they're not here or..." Or they don't want him after all. In case this is all an awful joke.

Ron gives him a kind smile. "Sure thing. I'll be here." He holds out his hand for a handshake.

Jason pauses for a second and then takes it. "Thanks," he says. He means for waiting but also for the other stuff. Jason knows looking after him hasn't been easy.

"Go on," Ron says.

Jason takes a deep breath and turns around. He marches up the little gravel path to the apartment building and presses the buzzer marked 17. That's the number Sunny gave him.

A voice crackles through the speaker. "Jason?"

"Yeah. It's me!" Jason sounds like a complete idiot, but the voice doesn't laugh.

The door buzzes, and Jason yanks it open. He hangs there for a moment, looking around the lobby. It's spacious and has ugly decor, like a motel from the eighties threw up. He shuffles awkwardly, waiting.

A person jogs into the space, holding out a hand. "Jason, bud! Nice to meet you finally. Sunny says you're the shit.

I'm Tucker, Sunny's cousin. *They them* pronouns."

"Uh..." Jason stumbles forward, reaching out to shake hands. "Good to meet you. Thanks for...uh, thanks for having me."

"Yeah, no worries. It's not a palace, but we make it work. C'mon up and meet the others," Tucker says, grinning.

They make their way up the stairs together, Tucker chatting away about the area, the coffee shops, the short walk to Commercial Drive. The trans-only swimming hour they go to every week at the local pool. Jason slowly starts to relax.

Tucker leads Jason down a hallway, then proudly stops in front of an apartment door. "Here we are. I think you're going to love it."

The door opens from inside, making Jason jump a little. Tucker doesn't laugh or anything, just introduces him.

"Jason, this is my partner, Alex. *He him* pronouns. Alex, this is Jason."

"Sunny's buddy!" The man who opened the door looks Jason up and down. "Any friend of the baby cousin is a friend of ours."

"Thanks for, uh, letting me crash here," says Jason. He follows Alex inside, looking around the spacious apartment.

"You're welcome." Alex leads the way to the living room. "And I remember what it was like when I was your age. Except my parents threw my tranny ass out." He laughs and then grins at Jason over his shoulder. "So we make our own family. It works out."

And for the first time, Jason feels like it might.

Tash McAdam is a Welsh-Canadian author of several books for young people. Tash identifies as trans and queer and uses the neutral pronoun *they*. As an English teacher, they are fully equipped to defend that grammar! They teach high-school English and computer science and have a couple of black belts in karate. They live in Vancouver.

orca soundings

For more information on all the books
in the Orca Soundings series, please visit
orcabook.com.